SPACE PENGUINS

PLANET PERIL!

For Owen, Georgina and Eliza. May their love of books give them wings. ~ **L A C**

For Brig ~ **J D**

STRIPES PUBLISHING
An imprint of Little Tiger Press
1 The Coda Centre, 189 Munster Road,
London SW6 6AW

A paperback original
First published in Great Britain in 2014

Text copyright © Lucy Courtenay, 2014
Illustrations copyright © James Davies, 2014
Cover illustration copyright © Antony Evans, 2014

ISBN: 978-1-84715-431-6

A CIP catalogue record for this book is available
from the British Library.

Printed and bound in the UK.

10 9 8 7 6 5 4 3 2 1

PLANET PERIL!

L A COURTENAY

**ILLUSTRATED BY
JAMES DAVIES**

MEET THE
SPACE
PENGUINS...

CAPTAIN:
Captain T. Krill
Emperor penguin
Height: 1.10m
Looks: yellow ear patches and
noble bearing
Likes: swordfish minus the
sword
Lab tests: showed leadership
qualities in fish challenge
Guaranteed to: keep calm in
a crisis

**FIRST MATE (ONCE UPON
A TIME):**
Beaky Wader, now known as
Dark Wader
Once Emperor penguin, now
part-robot
Height: 1.22m
Looks: shiny black armour
and evil laugh
Likes: prawn pizzas and ruling
the universe
Lab tests: cheated at every
challenge
Guaranteed to: cause trouble

PILOT (WITH NO SENSE OF DIRECTION):
Rocky Waddle
Rockhopper penguin
Height: 45cm
Looks: long yellow eyebrows
Likes: mackerel ice cream
Lab tests: fastest slider
in toboggan challenge
Guaranteed to: speed through
an asteroid belt while reading
charts upside down

SECURITY OFFICER AND HEAD CHEF:
Fuzz Allgrin
Little Blue penguin
Height: 33cm
Looks: small with fuzzy blue
feathers
Likes: fish fingers in cream and
truffle sauce
Lab tests: showed creativity
and aggression in ice-carving
challenge
Guaranteed to: defend ship,
crew and kitchen with his life

SHIP'S ENGINEER:
Splash Gordon
King penguin
Height: 95cm
Looks: orange ears and chest
markings
Likes: squid
Lab tests: solved ice-cube
challenge in under four
seconds
Guaranteed to: fix anything

LOADING...

Can we take off yet?

I am ICEcube, the mega-brainy computer guidance system for the *Tunafish*. But even though I have a brain the size of a moon, I can't fix the dents on the spaceship, or the cracked wing fins. I can't weld broken panels back together and I can't get burn marks off windscreens. Only four penguins in spacesuits can do that. I thank my circuit boards that I don't have a human crew.

A human crew was too expensive to train and send into deep space. Penguins were a lot cheaper. And they're better at this space stuff than you might think.

Last week, Rocky Waddle landed the damaged *Tunafish* here on the planet Chork. Although he did mean to land on the planet Cheez, next door.

Captain T. Krill made the Chorks and the Cheezis talk to each other for the first time in a thousand years, despite their many differences.

Splash Gordon invented the Chork2Cheez translating machine that made this possible.

And Fuzz Allgrin introduced the noble sport of fish-wrestling, which has turned into a major craze on both planets.

Chorks and Cheezis are now spending their time swapping fish-wrestling stories. Which is good, because the Chorks had just invented an enormous bomb that they were thinking of dropping on the Cheezis.

Phew!

We've been stuck on Chork for over a week now as the Space Penguins make the *Tunafish* space-ready again after an extremely close shave with the mechanical meteors of the planet Kroesus during our last adventure. You could say I was bored of waiting, except that computers can't feel bored.

By the way, I have counted all the stars in the universe twice now.

I wish they'd hurry up...

CHAPTER ONE

AN OOZI INVITATION

Captain Krill paced up and down the main cabin of the *Tunafish*, listening to the Intergalactic Space Report. It was quite difficult to hear because ICEcube was counting the number of stars in the universe out loud at the same time.

"Two billion, three hundred and three stars," ICEcube droned. "Two billion, three hundred and four stars…"

The Captain turned up the volume.

"…Two well known individuals have

been captured following a bold attempted robbery on the planet Kroesus. The Kroesan security forces turned the full might of the Tickling Stick of Justice on the suspects and forced a confession after only five minutes. Dark Wader, lately of the Death Starfish space station, and Anadin Skyporker, Emperor of the planet Sossij, can now look forward to years of imprisonment in the Kroesan high-security jail.

"In further news, the number of unusual alien species going missing from planets in section T of the universe has been climbing…"

The door from the engine room clanged shut as Splash Gordon, the *Tunafish*'s Chief Engineer, clumped into the cabin. Wriggling out of his penguin-sized spacesuit and helmet, Splash twanged up his goggles and wiped his feathered forehead. Then he twanged his goggles back down and wiped his forehead again, because his goggles had been in the way before.

"I've just heard some excellent news, Splash," Captain Krill beamed. "Beaky Wader and his pig-faced chum won't be chasing us for a while. They're facing prison sentences on the planet Kroesus."

"I'm glad to hear it," said Splash. "They almost destroyed our ship!"

"How's the *Tunafish* looking?" asked the Captain. "Can we leave yet?"

Splash counted out the *Tunafish*'s problems on his flippers. He quickly moved on to his webbed toes, as penguins only have two flippers.

"The nose cone was badly dented. The fins were covered in stress cracks. The propulsion system wasn't propelling properly. The boosters weren't boosting. And the windscreen was a total mess."

"But you've fixed all that," said Captain Krill. "Right?"

"I've reshaped the nose cone," Splash said. "Rocky has replaced the fins and sorted out the propulsion system."

Rocky Waddle came into the cabin, just behind Splash. "We're going to fly out of here so fast we might leave my eyebrows behind."

"The boosters and the windscreen?" Captain Krill checked.

A small blue penguin in a spacesuit slid into view on the outside of the windscreen, dangling upside down. He held up a cloth and some windscreen polish to the penguins inside the cabin.

"The boosters are boosting and the windscreen is shinier than your beak, Captain," Fuzz's voice said through the ship's intercom system.

"It's all systems go," Splash continued.

"Excellent," said Captain Krill. "The question is – all systems go *where*?"

"A nice holiday?" Rocky suggested. "There's a little planet tucked away in section V of the universe that looks penguin-friendly. According to the *Encyclopedia Galactica*, temperatures are low and its oceans are full of fish."

"Sounds perfect," said Captain Krill. "What are we waiting for?"

"The only problem is," Rocky added, "the fish are three times bigger than us. So we may have a little trouble catching and eating them."

"Ah," said Captain Krill.

"Two billion, three hundred and

thirty-seven stars," droned ICEcube. "Two billion—"

The computer's voice suddenly changed. "Incoming message, Captain. Stand by."

Captain Krill pricked up his ears. Fuzz waddled into the cabin and pulled off his helmet. The Space Penguins listened as ICEcube read out the message.

"'Chief Hubba Blubba of the planet Splurdj wishes to invite the Space Penguins as guests of honour to a feast to celebrate our Grand Opening tomorrow. We can't wait to meet you because you're so famous. We are sure you will love our planet.' End of message."

"Grand Opening of what?" said Splash.

"A tin of tuna would be nice," said Fuzz.

"A feast!" Rocky clapped his flippers. "I like being famous."

"ICEcube?" said Captain Krill. "What can you tell us about Splurdj?"

"Splurdj is a small, dark green planet orbiting an old red sun in section T of the universe," said ICEcube. "Its inhabitants are called Oozis. I understand they are dark green as well. Hubba Blubba recently got permission from the Intergalactic Planning Office to build a huge leisure complex. It will feature a cosmic crazy-golf course, a zoo, several restaurants and some top-of-the-range slime-skiing facilities."

"I'd like to see the restaurants," said Fuzz.

"It sounds AWESOME!" said Rocky. "Can we go?"

"Thank you for the information, ICEcube. Very helpful," said the Captain. "That explains the invitation. They must be opening their new leisure complex. I must say, it sounds very tempting."

"What about this Hubba Blubba? Is he friendly?" asked Splash.

"Of course he's friendly," said Rocky in surprise. "Only friendly aliens give out invitations."

"Not necessarily," said Splash.

"You worry too much," said Captain Krill. He smoothed his white tummy. "I like the sound of the slime-skiing myself. I think we should pop by."

"On it like a toboggan, Captain," said Rocky, waddling towards the flight panels. "ICEcube? Set the coordinates for Splurdj. It's time to PARTAY!"

CHAPTER TWO

SLIME TIME!

"ICEcube was right," said Fuzz, peering through the windscreen as Rocky steered the *Tunafish* through the atmosphere of the planet Splurdj. "It IS dark green."

Splurdj hung below them like a large rolled-up bogey. Except for the places where the red sunlight turned it brown, it was green all over. It wasn't the prettiest planet the Space Penguins had ever seen.

"Cleared for landing, *Tunafish*," came a voice over the intercom. "Welcome to

Splurdj, planet of fun."

"We'll be the judge of that," said Splash.

"Whoa!" Rocky said in alarm, fighting to keep the *Tunafish* straight as the wheels skidded sideways on the landing strip.

The spaceship spun round a couple of times and slid to a stop.

The Space Penguins smoothed their feathers and peered out at a rocky-looking building at the end of the strip.

BHARGH-BRUP BHARGH-BRUP
BHARRRGH-BHARRGH-BRRRUP…

"What's that noise?" said Captain Krill.

"Oozi trumpets," said ICEcube. "The
traditional instrument of Splurdj."

The Space Penguins looked more
closely. A welcoming committee of dark
green Oozis were standing by the rocky
building, holding floppy-looking tubes
above their heads and whirling them
round and round.

BHARRRGH-BHARRGH-BRRRUP
went the Oozi trumpets.

"They sound exactly like those elephant seals that lived next to us back in the zoo," said Fuzz. "They were always breaking wind on their ice floe."

"Excellent," said Rocky. He made a farting sound with his flipper.

"Everyone on their best behaviour," said Captain Krill, as the others sniggered. "We mustn't offend our hosts."

The crew climbed out of the *Tunafish* and tried not to slip on the slimy landing-strip surface. Then they waddled carefully over to meet the welcoming committee. The largest, ooziest Oozi held his long green and yellow arms towards them.

"Welcome!" he squelched. "Welcome, Captain Thrill, Rocky Puddle, Fuzz Allchin, Splat Gordon! I am Hubba

Blubba, Chief Oozi of the planet Splurdj.
I can't believe I'm meeting you at last!"

Fuzz nudged the *Tunafish*'s pilot. "I'm
going to call you Rocky Puddle from now
on."

"Getting a bit fat under the beak,
Allchin?" Rocky teased
back.

"It's Splash," said
Splash. "Not Splat.
And Captain T.
Krill."

"I apologize!"
said Hubba Blubba.
"What does the T
stand for?"

"Trustworthy," said
Captain Krill.

The Space Penguins looked at the
Captain in amazement. He had never told
them that.

"Anyway," said Captain Krill, blushing a little. "Thank you for inviting us, your Ooziness."

Hubba Blubba bowed. Captain Krill bowed back.

It's not easy for penguins to bow, especially when their feet are on a slippery surface. The Captain tipped forward completely. The Space Penguins rushed to help him back on to his feet.

Rushing was a bad idea. They slipped over as well.

"Whoops," said Hubba Blubba. "You'll find sliding easier than walking on Splurdj with those funny little legs of yours. Let us enter Fort Gundj and make our way to the feast!"

BHARGH-BRUP BHARGH-BRUP BHARRRGH-BHARRGH-BRRRUP went the Oozi trumpets.

Hubba Blubba glided away into the depths of the rocky building, followed by the rest of the welcoming committee. The Space Penguins lay on their tummies and whizzed after them, pushing themselves along with their flippers.

"I'm starving," Rocky said, as they zoomed down a rocky corridor.

"Me too," said Fuzz.

The corridor ended at a large green cavern decorated with twinkling red lights. The Space Penguins had got up such a good speed along the slimy floor that they almost crashed into Hubba Blubba as he stopped at the cavern mouth.

The Chief Oozi spread out his long green and yellow arms. "Oozis!" he cried. "Let us welcome our guests, the famous Space Penguins!"

Long tables lined with clapping Oozis stretched before the penguins. The sound of wet applause and farty Oozi trumpets echoed around the cavern.

"This place is growing on me," said Rocky, as they slid down the entrance ramp behind their host.

"Like mould," said Splash darkly.

Hubba Blubba led the penguins up to a long table on a raised platform.

"You are the first non-Oozis to see the work we have done on Splurdj," he said cheerfully. "After the feast I will show you around our paradise planet. Help yourselves to some spewkrangle stew."

The Space Penguins looked doubtfully at the large bowls of sticky green stuff in the middle of the table. Spewkrangle stew looked and smelled like rotten snot.

"We don't have spoons," said Rocky.

"Or plates," added the Captain.

Hubba Blubba roared with laughter. "No one ever told me the great Space Penguins were so funny!"

He dipped a green and yellow finger into the spewkrangle stew. There was a horrible slurping sound and to the penguins' astonishment, the level of stew in the big bowl began to sink.

"I'd always thought it was a myth that there were creatures in the universe that used their mouths both to talk AND eat," said Hubba Blubba, as his finger slurped up the green goo like a straw. "But I see it all the time in my Space Zoo. Such peculiar habits! It's fascinating. Eat up!"

"I'm actually still quite full from breakfast," said Fuzz.

Captain Krill politely dipped his flipper in the spewkrangle stew and sat there for a bit, making "yummy!" noises.

Hubba Blubba drained the rest. As he lifted his finger out of the bowl, it shivered and went BWAAAA.

"Did his finger just burp?" said Splash to Rocky.

"Double awesome," said Rocky.

The farty trumpets rang out. There was a sudden loud whoop somewhere up in the cavern roof.

"Let the entertainment begin!" announced Hubba Blubba.

Four green, slimy acrobats swung through the hall on long red ropes high above the dinner guests, scattering slime as they went. The one at the front wore a black crown with sparkly green bits.

"Woo hoo!" they cried, as they spun and twirled.

Splash quietly wiped a bit of slime off his beak.

Hubba Blubba clapped hard. "The one with the crown is Glog," he informed the penguins. "The Glogettes are the finest acrobats in Splurdj. Look at them fly!"

The Glogettes balanced on each other's shoulders. They spun on each other's heads. They made the audience gasp with amazement as they bent their slippery bodies into impossible shapes.

"Not bad," muttered Fuzz when at last the Glogettes took their bows and slid away. "If flying bogies are your thing."

"We will now tour Splurdj's many delights by Gooter," said Hubba Blubba. "Gooters are vehicles of Oozi design. You'll like them. Follow me!"

CHAPTER THREE

A TOUR OF SPLURDJ

Outside, the Space Penguins found a green, saucer-shaped vehicle hovering above the slippery ground.

"This," said Hubba Blubba, "is a Gooter."

"How does it stay up?" asked Splash, peering underneath.

FWPWPWPWPWP. A gust of stinky green smoke exploded from the Gooter's three thrusters, nearly knocking Splash backwards.

"Oozi gas," said Hubba Blubba. "One

hundred per cent natural. We extract it from our own bodies and store it in tanks. We are a resourceful species."

He squeezed into the Gooter beside the Space Penguins, who were all feeling as green as the Oozi gas. With another FWPWPWPWP the Gooter rose into the air.

The Splurdj landscape rolled away beneath them, green and slimy, as the Gooter veered towards a range of mountains.

"The Mountains of Mush," said Hubba Blubba, waving at the slopes below. "Slime-skiing is our favourite sport here on Splurdj."

Hubba Blubba explained how it worked. You went to the top of a mountain and zoomed down on your back, head first. Because you couldn't see where you were going, you had no idea what you might bump into. It was wonderfully dangerous.

"Can we have a go?" said Rocky eagerly.

"No time, alas!" said Hubba Blubba.
"Oozis hold the intergalactic speed record
for speed sliding, you know. Two hundred
and thirty-three zonkometres an hour!
And down there you will see our cosmic
crazy-golf course."

The Space Penguins looked at the
transparent dome beneath them. A couple
of Oozis with clubs floated and spun in
slow circles inside, sometimes hitting balls
through hoops and sometimes not.

Way below, the penguins could see the *Tunafish* parked sideways on the landing strip beside Fort Gundj as the Gooter banked with one more FWPWPWPWP towards a huge glass dome.

"Wow!" said Fuzz. "It's so colourful!"

The Space Penguins admired the blue waters, the yellow and red flowers, the bright green trees, the pink elevated pathways and the large white iceberg in the heart of the dome.

GRAND OPENING TOMORROW!

"My Space Zoo," said Hubba Blubba proudly, as the Gooter glided overhead. "Every possible habitat for every possible creature. I have spent my life collecting the animal wonders of the universe. I even have a Wangflang."

"What's a Wangflang?" asked Fuzz.

"One of the most dangerous creatures in the cosmos!"

"Can we go inside?" Captain Krill asked hopefully. "If we can't try slime-skiing, I'd love to slide down that iceberg instead."

"Of course!" promised the Oozi chief. "But first we have work to do. Something that only the famous Space Penguins can help me with."

Rocky preened his eyebrows. "You've picked the right guys. Black and white, full of might, faster than the speed of light. That's us."

"I'm blue," Fuzz said, a little crossly.

"Who lives on the massive iceberg?" asked Splash, looking again at the gleaming white mountain.

Hubba Blubba gave a strange smile. "Some truly remarkable creatures," he said. "Now, this part of the tour is over, my waddling friends. Let us return to Fort Gundj."

As the Gooter did a big loop right around the dome, Splash noticed a banner hung above a large set of doors, which read "GRAND OPENING TOMORROW!"

They landed on the ground outside Fort Gundj. But this time Hubba Blubba went past the dining cavern and turned left into a narrow passage. BHARGH-BRUP BHARGH-BRUP BHARRRGH-BHARRGH-BRRRUP went the Oozi trumpets.

"Guys," said Splash, as they slid after

their host on their bellies. "Something about that Space Zoo makes me nervous."

"It looks brilliant," said Fuzz.

"Do you think the creatures Hubba Blubba mentioned would mind us having a go on their iceberg?" Rocky said.

"I'm sure he'd put them inside their cages for a while, if we asked him nicely," said Captain Krill.

They whizzed along until a metal door slid open and they found themselves inside a small, circular room. Unlike the gloomy dining cavern, it was brightly lit and modern. Computer screens shone on the walls and Oozi technicians sat at steel desks, pressing buttons. The Oozi musicians stood outside the door in dripping rows with their trumpets dangling by their sides.

"This is where I control everything in my zoo." Hubba Blubba pointed at the screens.

"Tell me, what is your perfect habitat?"

"Cold," said Rocky.

"Slippery," said Fuzz.

"Penguins are simple creatures," said Captain Krill. "Give us water and sub-zero temperatures and we're happy."

"Just as I thought," said Hubba Blubba. "Does your perfect habitat look something like … this?"

The biggest screen showed the large iceberg in the centre of the dome.

"Yes!" cried Fuzz.

"That's it exactly!" said the Captain.

Rocky imagined getting up to speeds
of at least two hundred and thirty-three
zonkometres an hour down the iceberg.
He could smash that intergalactic speed-
sliding record if he tried.

"Guys," said Splash. "We ought to go.
We've got that Thing. Remember?"

"What Thing?" said Captain Krill.

"You're talking tail-rot, Splash," said
Rocky. "We haven't got a Thing."

"Tell me," Hubba Blubba said
delicately. "Your favourite food is?"

"Fish fingers in cream and truffle sauce," said Fuzz.

"We really do have a Thing," said Splash, a bit louder.

The others ignored him.

"And your best trick is?" said Hubba Blubba, in the same delicate voice.

"'I'm pretty good at juggling clams," said Rocky. "As long as there's only one."

"Hmm. Doesn't sound very entertaining," said Hubba Blubba with a frown. "We'll have to teach you something else."

"Why do you want to teach us stuff?" said Fuzz in surprise.

"Because you are going to be the prize exhibits in my Space Zoo," explained Hubba Blubba with a slimy smile.

Too late, the penguins realized the horrible truth.

"It's a trap!" roared Splash. "Waddle for your lives!"

The Oozi musicians barred the exit. Their floppy trumpets suddenly looked threatening.

Laser beams then criss-crossed the room in a burst of red light, scanning the space heroes' bodies – flipper to flipper, back of neck to top of head, tummies to toes. Everything was measured in swift flashes of red, and numbers streamed on the screens around the Space Penguins.

Then the lasers vanished. A big red net dropped from the ceiling and tightened around the *Tunafish*'s crew, hoisting them into the air.

"Hey, blubberbrain!" roared Fuzz, struggling to get free. "Put me down or risk the rage of the Fuzzmeister!"

"I'm upside down!" complained Rocky. "My eyebrows will be ruined."

"I told you we had a Thing!" shouted Splash. "We should have left AS SOON

AS I MENTIONED THE THING!"

"This isn't on, Hubba Blubba," said Captain Krill angrily. "It goes against every rule in the book!"

"I don't care about rules," Hubba Blubba grinned. "I just care about my Space Zoo. My collection is now complete. Dear Space Penguins, I knew inviting you to Splurdj was my best idea ever. You are the spew in my stew. The trail on my snail. You are MINE FOREVER!"

CHAPTER FOUR

CAPTURED!

No matter how hard the Space Penguins struggled, they couldn't get free. The red net held them as tight as tinned sardines.

A hatch flipped open in the Control Room ceiling.

"You won't get away with this!" Captain Krill roared.

"I just did," Hubba Blubba chortled. "You will be transported straight to my Space Zoo, to that big iceberg you admired

a few minutes ago. Remember those
remarkable creatures I mentioned? That's
YOU. I built that habitat just for YOU, and
it's perfect – you told me so yourselves.
Dinner will be along shortly. So will an
instructor, to teach you some decent
tricks. There's nothing more boring than
zoo creatures that can't do tricks. See you
tomorrow for the Grand Opening!"

"Slimeball!" Fuzz bellowed, as the
penguins were hoisted through the hatch
and into the dull evening light outside.
"Bogey-bum! GUNGE-GUTS!"

The Space Penguins twirled
sickeningly in mid-air as the Control
Room hatch disappeared from view.
Then they swung and lurched towards
the top of the great dome. Now
they could see that they were attached
to a huge green crane, almost
invisible against the green, slimy rocks

of Fort Gundj. The whole thing felt like a funfair ride – only it was no fun at all.

A hole opened up in the top of the dome and the Space Penguins looked down at their new home. The red net was lowered through the hole until the penguins' feet – and Rocky's head – touched solid ground. They were at the very top of the iceberg in the centre of the Space Zoo.

The net released them. Rocky tipped sideways, landing on his belly and started sliding down the iceberg, away from the rest of the crew.

"Whoo!" he cried, gathering speed.

"That looks brilliant," said Captain Krill, watching Rocky go.

"We've been captured by a stinky slime beast," said Splash. "We're doomed to stay in this place for the rest of our lives, and you call it brilliant?"

Captain Krill tore his eyes away from the icy slope. "You're right, of course, Splash. It isn't brilliant at all."

"It's an OUTRAGE," bellowed Fuzz.

"Luckily for us," said Splash, lifting his belly to reveal an egg-shaped toolbox, "I had my suspicions before we landed. I tucked my toolbox on top of my feet when we left the *Tunafish*. If I can construct some means of winching us back up to the hatch again..."

"Wheeeeeee!" said Fuzz, hurling himself down the iceberg.

"I'd better go after him," said Captain Krill.

Fuzz and the Captain streaked away down the glittering white slope.

"Oh, hairy haddocks," sighed Splash. He covered up his toolbox, lay on his belly and raced after the others.

The penguins landed at the bottom
of the iceberg, beaks almost touching the
water, and picked themselves up.

"I want to do it again!" shouted Rocky.

Splash folded his flippers and tapped
one foot. "How, exactly?"

Fuzz waddled speedily up the iceberg.
He got about halfway before he came
tumbling down again.

"That's what I call a one-way
experience," he said, brushing himself
down.

"So the escape plan you mentioned,
Splash," said Captain Krill. "The one about
using your toolbox to build something
from the top of the iceberg to the hatch in
the top of the dome. I'm guessing we can't
do that now?"

Splash's foot was still tapping. "You
guessed right."

"So we shouldn't have slid down the

iceberg in the first place," said Fuzz.

"Nope," said Splash.

"But it was awesome," said Rocky.

"Tremendous," said Captain Krill.

"Mega," said Fuzz.

"Look," said Splash.

A big holographic sign was projected near the base of the iceberg. Red letters spelled out the words:

PENGRINS:
Marine creatures from an unknown planet with unknown talents.

Rocky tossed his eyebrows in disgust. "There's nothing unknown about my talents."

"They've spelled penguins wrong," added Splash.

"They have?" said Fuzz.

"Right," said the Captain, clapping his flippers to get their attention. "We're on an icy island in the middle of a Space Zoo.

In order to escape, we have two options. Swim across the water to the next island, and the next, and the next, until we reach the edge of the dome."

"Then what?" asked Splash.

"We break out," said Captain Krill. "Somehow…"

"What's the second option?" Fuzz asked.

Captain Krill looked up at the elevated pink pathways, criss-crossing the dome. "Learn to fly," he said.

"WHAT?" said the others.

"That could take a while," said Splash, glancing at his stubby flippers.

"I think those pathways are for visitors looking around the zoo," the Captain explained. "If we could just get up there we could waddle all the way to the doors."

Fuzz flexed his flippers and pointed his toes. "Swimming it is. What are we waiting for?"

The penguins flung themselves into the water.

"If there's one thing I love more than sliding," said Rocky, bobbing to the surface, "it's swimming. Which way, Captain?"

Captain Krill had no time to answer. A huge, steel-clawed tentacle broke the surface just in front of him, followed by another, and another.

SNAP! SNAP! SNAP!

"OW!" roared Captain Krill, as one of the steel claws pulled a clump of feathers out of his tail. "Back to shore! NOW!"

More tentacles exploded upwards, waving in the air. Captain Krill shot out of the water like a cork from a bottle. The others followed. They landed hard on the icy ground, shocked and shaking.

The penguins exchanged horrified looks.

What the flaming fish guts was THAT?

CHAPTER FIVE

THE GREAT FLIP

"I think I just died," Rocky panted, lying back on the ice. "Someone kick me to prove I'm alive. OW! Thanks, Fuzz. OW! Hey, no need to kick me twice!"

"If you hadn't slid down the iceberg, Splash would be sorting our escape through the top of the dome!" shouted Fuzz. "Instead we nearly got eaten alive!"

"I lost my balance!" Rocky protested. "What's *your* excuse?"

"That octopus thing was an impressive

piece of technology," said Splash, changing the subject.

The penguins could see nothing beneath the dark blue waters.

Fuzz dabbled a toe.

WHOOOSH!

A great silver claw shot out of the water and nearly snapped Fuzz's beak off. The penguins fell backwards in shock.

Captain Krill got to his feet for the second time, rubbing the bald patch on his tail. "We need to think," he said.

FWPWPWP.

A Gooter was buzzing towards them.

"Escape is impossible," boomed a female Oozi over the Gooter's loudspeaker. "Enter the water again and the ClawBorg will rip you to shreds."

A hatch in the Gooter's belly opened and a bucket was lowered down. It landed on the iceberg with a clink.

"Fish fingers in cream and truffle sauce!" Fuzz gasped, peering inside the bucket.

"I hate fish fingers," sulked Rocky. "You should have said we liked mackerel ice cream."

"Or squid," said Splash.

"Or swordfish," said the Captain. "Minus the sword."

Fuzz leaped on the fish fingers. After one bite, he spat them out.

"URGH," he said, wiping his beak. "They look like fish fingers but they're basically spewkrangle stew covered in crumbs and white slime."

FWPWPWP.

Now a long, thin plank was lowered through the hatch. An Oozi in a black and green crown was balancing on top, holding a box in her arms.

"Greetings," said the Oozi. She slid on to the ice with a squelch and put down the box. "We have a lot of work to do."

"You're that acrobat from the feast," said Fuzz. "Glog!"

"You were great," said Rocky. "You know, for a flying bag of gunge."

Glog gave a slippery bow.

"Get back into your smelly Gooter and buzz off," said Captain Krill.

The other penguins looked shocked.

"Flying fishcakes, Captain, that's a bit rude," said Rocky.

"I apologize," said Captain Krill. "But I am extremely angry about all this."

"There's no point complaining," said Glog. "You're here to stay. I am here on Chief Oozi's orders, to teach you some tricks. Tricks will make your life more fun. Tricks will get you more food. Tricks are the key to happiness in this zoo. Now, you will do what I say or I will throw you to the ClawBorg. Are we clear?"

The penguins eyed the water. They could see the steel tentacles of the ClawBorg waving around just beneath the waves.

"Clear as icecubes," said Splash.

Glog flipped open the box and pulled out some juggling balls, a long rope and four frilly-necked outfits.

"These are your costumes," said Glog. "They have been designed especially for you and will fit perfectly. Put them on."

"But they're dresses!" said Rocky.

"They're pink and sparkly!" said Fuzz.

"I summon the ClawBorg—" Glog began in a loud voice.

"Put the frocks on, team!" ordered Captain Krill, as the water rippled in an ominous manner.

The penguins reluctantly did as they were told.

"Chief Oozi said one of you could juggle," said Glog.

Rocky picked up one of the juggling balls and threw it up and down a couple of times. He dropped it almost straight away.

"Practice makes perfect," said Glog. "Now, the rope is for skipping."

She demonstrated, covering the rope with slime. She thrust the rope at Fuzz. "Give it a go, titch."

Fuzz went bright red with rage. "Call me that again and I'll throw YOU to the ClawBorg!"

Ignoring him, Glog unhooked the long, thin plank from the still-hovering Gooter. Then, using the costume box as a pivot, she balanced the plank on top.

"A see-saw?" muttered Rocky. "You have to be squidding."

Glog climbed on to one end of the see-saw.

"I want someone to jump on the other end. You," she said, pointing at Captain Krill. "The fat one."

Captain Krill looked behind him for a fat penguin.

"She means you, Captain," said Splash, sniggering a bit.

"No," said Captain Krill furiously.

"I summon the ClawBorg—"

"I am only doing this because I have no choice," Captain Krill grumbled.

He waddled up to the other end of the see-saw and jumped.

PING!

Glog did a backflip and landed on the ice with the kind of slap you get when you drop a water balloon on the ground. The penguins were splattered in slime.

"The Great Flip," said Glog. "Your turn."

"Never!" growled Fuzz.

"No way, stingray," said Rocky.

"I think … we should give it a go," said Captain Krill thoughtfully.

The Space Penguins stared at their leader. Why had he suddenly changed his tune?

Captain Krill turned to Glog. "Thank you for your instructions. We will practise until we are perfect."

"If you get this right, Hubba Blubba will reward you," Glog said, looking pleased. "And I'll get extra helpings of spewkrangle stew for breakfast," she added, as the Gooter winched her up again. The hatch shut and it jetted off in a cloud of stinky gas.

The four space mates ripped off their pink frilly costumes as fast as they could. Rocky stomped on his.

"You're insane, Captain," said Fuzz, hurling his skipping rope away. "Why did you say we'd practise?"

"You didn't even say we'd 'mullet' over," said Rocky. "Get it?"

"The Great Flip is about to become the Great Escape," said Captain Krill. "If we get it right, we can flip ourselves over the water, over the ClawBorg and on to the next island."

"Wow," said Splash. "Why didn't I think of that?"

The penguins patted Captain Krill on the back and high-flippered each other.

The Captain gazed at his belly and frowned. "I'm not that fat," he said.

CHAPTER SIX

BATTLE WITH THE CLAWBORG

The penguins took turns to practise the Great Flip in order of size – Rocky flipped Fuzz, Splash flipped Rocky, Captain Krill flipped Splash. Then they practised flipping each other in twos and threes. After a particularly high flip, Rocky accidentally kicked over a surveillance camera mounted on a pole by the water's edge.

"Good riddance," said Fuzz, waving cheerfully as the camera bubbled and sank.

"Now let's see if we can do it with three of you at one end and me doing the flipping," suggested the Captain.

This took a lot more practice. The penguins skidded, fell, bent their flippers in half, twisted their toes, and somersaulted over and over. Finally, they flopped on to the ice and took a break. They were starving by now, and forced themselves to eat some of the horrible "fish fingers".

"There's a really weird creature on the jungly island opposite," said Splash, as he caught sight of something moving between the trees. "Seriously. It's blue with a head like a balloon."

"It must be thinking, *Who are those handsome creatures on that iceberg? I wish I looked like them*," said Rocky.

"Hubba Blubba probably kidnapped it as well," said Captain Krill. He frowned. "Remember the Intergalactic Space Report said creatures had been going missing from this section of the universe."

"Old Hubba Blubberchops is one slimy customer," said Fuzz.

Captain Krill finished his "fish finger" and wiped his beak with his flipper. "We'll put the see-saw as close to the water as we can. I'll flip you guys out of here."

"Who's going to flip you, Captain?" asked Splash.

"Don't worry. I have a plan."

Fuzz climbed on Rocky's shoulders, and Rocky climbed on Splash's shoulders. They balanced carefully as Captain Krill took a long waddle-up and jumped.

The three penguins did three perfect somersaults over the water and into the undergrowth opposite. The ClawBorg didn't stir.

Rocky jumped up first, brushing leaves out of his eyebrows. "We did it!" he shouted. "Rockhopper on!"

"What's your plan, Captain?" Splash called.

"I'm going to fly," Captain Krill shouted back.

He moved the pivot, turning the see-saw into a ramp. Then he waddled as far up the iceberg as he could, lay on his belly and pushed hard with his flippers. Reaching the ramp, he zoomed up and soared above the water with his wings outstretched. But he didn't soar far enough.

SPLOSHHH!

The ClawBorg exploded from the water. The Captain started swimming for his life, struggling between its steel tentacles.

"We're coming, Captain!" roared Fuzz, leaping into the churning water. "Hold on!" Rocky and Splash dived in after him.

SLAM! A tentacle missed Splash by millimetres.

SLAM! The ClawBorg whacked Fuzz like a cricket ball, sending the little penguin up into the air.

"Try that again and I'll turn you into ClawBorg soup!" roared Fuzz, landing back in the water with a plop.

The penguins darted among the ClawBorg's thrashing tentacles. The water heaved and boiled. The ClawBorg grabbed in every direction, tying itself into an enormous knot. The claws on its horribly tangled tentacles clattered furiously, but the penguins were out of reach.

The triumphant penguins leaped on to the shoreline of the jungly island.

"TRIPLE awesome!" gasped Rocky. "We knotted the ClawBorg!"

"It may unknot itself quicker than we think," said the Captain. "Get waddling, crew. We have to cross this island and get into the water on the other side before it's too late."

The jungly habitat was horribly hot. Within five minutes, the penguins were sweating. It was nearly impossible to waddle through the thick undergrowth.

"I feel like a soggy hankie," puffed Fuzz. Moisture dripped off his beak. "Can we stop? You know, so we can breathe?"

Something crashed out of the undergrowth. Something tall and thin and blue, with long toes and a balloon-shaped head. It stared at the Space Penguins with

big, dark eyes. The Space Penguins stared
back.

"Shivering shrimps," said Rocky.

"It looked smaller from our iceberg,"
said Splash.

The balloon beast made a funny noise.
"EEEE!"

"Did its head just get smaller?" asked
Fuzz.

"EEEE!" went the balloon beast.
Its head shrank a little more.

"I wish my head did that," said Rocky admiringly.

"So do we," said Splash. "Your head's way too big."

A hologram sign shimmered among the trees.

"'AIREE'," read Fuzz. "'A rare mammal from Arcturon III, the Airee can inflate its head and fly short distances.'"

The balloon creature's head was tiny now. It bent over and nibbled daintily at the vegetation by the penguins' feet.

"I guess you're an Airee," the Captain said.

Splash patted the Airee's side. It seemed to like it.

"Do you want to escape?" Splash asked. "With us?"

The Airee's head started inflating again, until it was so full of air that the creature started rising off the ground.

"Grab its feet!" Captain Krill said. "It might float us on to that elevated walkway!" He pointed to the pink path stretching high above their heads like a strand of bubblegum, from one side of the dome to the other.

The penguins leaped up and grasped at the creature's long toes with their flippers. Hanging on as tightly as they could, they let the Airee lift them gently off the ground.

But the Airee didn't have enough air to reach the pathway. It sailed down again, over a high fence dividing the jungle island in half, and landed on a wide white beach on the other side.

The penguins gazed sadly across the water in front of them. In the distance they could see a grey rocky patch of land lying next to the glass walls of the dome.

"EEEE!" said the Airee apologetically.

"You did your best," said Splash, patting it before turning to the others. "The Airee can only fly short distances, it said so on the sign."

"Looks like we'll have to swim after all," said Captain Krill. "And hope the ClawBorg is still tied up."

"Ouch!" yelped Rocky, as he stepped into a hole concealed beneath the undergrowth. "Give us a flipper, I'm stuck."

"'POMPOMS'," read Captain Krill, as another holographic sign appeared. "'Red-furred mammals from Azimus Pi that live in burrows.'"

"Silly place to put a burrow," Rocky complained, as the Captain tugged him free. "Right under my feet."

A dozen small, furry red creatures came scuttling out at once. They gathered around Splash.

"Aren't they adorable!" said Splash, leaning down to stroke one. "We can't leave them behind, Captain."

"We'll give them a ride across the water," said the Captain. "But what about the Airee?"

"Its head should keep it afloat," said Splash. "Like armbands do."

Splash, Captain Krill and Rocky held out their flippers for the PomPoms to climb aboard. Two PomPoms sat on Rocky's head, clinging to his eyebrows.

"Ready, team?" said Captain Krill, preparing to dive in. "Then let's go!"

CHAPTER SEVEN

THE WANGFLANG

Hubba Blubba had just finished a large supper. He glided into his Control Room, full of good humour and spewkrangle stew, to enjoy the sight of his newly captured penguins.

The screen showing the penguins' iceberg was dark.

He tapped the screen crossly. "Where's my penguin-cam?"

"It got broken when they were practising a trick," said the Oozi

technician operating the cameras. "We're
sending someone to fix it in a minute."

"Send them NOW! I want to see those
penguins playing! Eating! Doing tricks!"

A sudden movement on another screen
caught Hubba Blubba's eye. The slimy
alien goggled at the sight of four penguins,
a dozen PomPoms and an Airee swimming
away from the jungle island. Where was
the ClawBorg? How had the penguins got
so far from their iceberg without being
captured? And why were they stealing his
Airee and his adorable PomPoms?

"Let's see how those penguins get on with my next watery surprise," he said, narrowing his eyes. "Activate the Wipeout Wave!"

"You'll drown them if you do that, Chief," said the technician in alarm.

"Press the button," ordered Hubba Blubba. "No one escapes from my Space Zoo the day before my Grand Opening!"

The Space Penguins were halfway to the grey rocky habitat when sirens began to wail. They turned their heads and stared in horror at the great wall of water racing up behind them as they swam.

"Tsunami!" gasped Rocky.

"Bless you," said Fuzz.

"Swim faster!" shouted Captain Krill.

It was too late. With a ghastly roar, the enormous wave swept them up.

The penguins, the PomPoms and the
Airee spun and tumbled through the water.

Fuzz was the first to surface, riding
the Airee like a jet ski. "We are the Space
Penguins, hear us FLAP!" he shouted.

The PomPoms on Rocky's head were
using his eyebrows as reins. Five more
were riding on the Captain's back, clinging
on to each other and squealing.

"Sprats away!" cried Splash, surfing
on his belly beside the Captain and Rocky
with four passengers
balanced on his
back.

With a mighty CRASH, the Wipeout Wave hurled them all down on to the rocky shoreline. Breathless and wet, the penguins tumbled beak over flippers and landed – PLONK – upside down in front of a big grey rock.

"What a ride!" shouted Fuzz above the sirens, clapping his flippers.

"EEEE!" said the Airee.

The PomPoms huddled into a tight ball, then exploded upwards in a triumphant shower of wet red fluff.

"That's a great trick," said Rocky enviously. "These little guys make my clam juggling look pretty lame."

There was a slithering noise behind the rock. The penguins looked round.

"What in the name of smoked salmon is THAT?" said the Captain.

The creature facing them looked like an angry two-headed crocodile, with fierce red eyes and enormous black teeth. Its black coat shimmered like a slick of oil.

"Uh-oh," said Splash. He pointed to the big hologram sign projected beside the rock.

WANGFLANG:
One of the most dangerous creatures in the cosmos, the Wangflang breathes fire and enjoys causing destruction.

The sirens suddenly went quiet. Hubba Blubba's voice boomed over the loudspeakers.

"Calling the Space Penguins. All I wanted was for you to enjoy yourselves in my Space Zoo. You have ruined tomorrow's Grand Opening. As my Wipeout Wave failed to drown you, my Wangflang will finish you off. Then I shall turn your iceberg into a slime-skiing mountain. You were a big disappointment."

"No weedy Wangflang can finish off the Fuzzmeister," said Fuzz, as the loudspeaker went quiet again.

The Wangflang roared. Two blasts of fire exploded by the penguins' feet. The Airee inflated its head in alarm and took off, while the PomPoms scattered.

"Does anyone have a plan?" asked Rocky.

"Look," said Splash.

The PomPoms had gathered beside the glass walls of the dome and were digging a hole in the sand.

"A tunnel!" gasped the Captain. "Flippers to attention, penguins. We just need to keep the Wangflang busy."

"No problem," said Fuzz. "CHAARGE!"

He waddled up the big grey rock, did a somersault in mid-air and landed on the Wangflang's back. The beast bellowed in outrage and belched fire from both mouths at once. The jaws on its two heads snapped like traps.

"Can't get me up here, can you?" Fuzz called out. "Take that, bonfire breath!"

WHACK, WHACK, WHACK went Fuzz's tiny flippers.

The Wangflang roared again, flames shooting out from its mouths. Rocky's eyebrows caught alight, and he rushed into the water to put them out.

With a sudden toss of its long spiky tail, the Wangflang sent Fuzz flying. Captain Krill and Splash dragged Fuzz out of the way as two jets of fire blasted into the ground, leaving smoking holes.

Rocky gave the Wangflang's tail a good kick. "That's for messing with the brows!"

The Wangflang opened its mouths, preparing to blast the penguins to charcoal.

The Space Penguins raced out of the way, shielding their heads with their flippers, as fire scorched the glass dome wall in long brown streaks.

"Too close," gasped Rocky.

Splash lifted his belly and opened the egg-shaped toolbox on his feet.

"How did you keep hold of that?" said Fuzz. "We just swam through a tsunami!"

"Glue," said Splash. He pulled out a catapult and picked up a jagged stone from the ground. "Let's try this."

TWANG!

The Wangflang gave an ear-shattering shriek of pain and anger as the stone struck it on the side of its head.

"My turn!" said Rocky, taking the catapult from Splash. He scooped up some rocks and took aim.

TWANG! TWANG!

This time the stones struck the Wangflang's eyes. It stumbled about, lashing its tail like a whip.

Meanwhile, the PomPoms were digging so fast, the penguins could hardly see them through the flying sand. At last, the little creatures jumped into the hole and popped up on the other side of the glass dome, slime and sand coating their red fur.

"Any minute…" Captain Krill panted, dodging the Wangflang's claws as the last of the PomPoms disappeared into the tunnel. "Now!"

As the smallest, Fuzz went first, leaping into the hole after the PomPoms. Then Rocky. Then Splash. Last of all, the Captain. Behind them, the Wangflang gave a mad howl of rage.

"Shame they didn't make the hole bigger," said Rocky, as the Captain's belly got stuck halfway through.

The penguins grabbed on to the Captain's flippers. "On three," said Rocky. "One, two, three – pull!"

Captain Krill sucked in his tummy. With a POP, the others pulled him through the hole.

The four penguins collapsed in a cool puddle of slime. It felt wonderful on their singed feathers. They high-flippered each other and stroked the excited PomPoms by their feet, then high-flippered each other again. They were free!

CHAPTER EIGHT

TO THE RESCUE!

Up in the Control Room, Hubba Blubba was in a filthy temper. He had been watching his ClawBorg, which was still out of action despite the technicians' best efforts. Now he was back at the Wangflang screen, and the Space Penguins were nowhere to be seen.

Glog slid into the Control Room, looking worried.

"I have come to apologize," she said, with a low bow. "I think the penguins used the Great Flip to escape from their iceberg.

I had no idea my trick would be used in such an underhand way."

"Never mind that," said Hubba Blubba crossly. "The Wangflang just ate them and I missed it. I wanted to hear the crunch of his jaws on their ungrateful penguin heads."

On the screen, the Wangflang paced up and down, shrieking and blasting fire.

"I can't see any bones or beaks, Chief," said Glog. "Are you sure the Wangflang ate them?"

Hubba Blubba tapped the screen. "If it didn't eat them … they must have escaped. AGAIN," he said. "But not for long."

Tongues of Wangflang fire blasted through the hole under the dome wall as the penguins hastily filled it in and patted the earth down firmly. The PomPoms did their huddle-and-explode move in celebration.

"There's no way that Wangflang can follow us now!" said Rocky in relief.

The Airee was still floating inside the walls of the dome, gazing sadly at them with its big dark eyes.

"We forgot the Airee!" Splash gasped. "We have to go back!"

"Yay!" said Fuzz. He started digging again.

"You crazy crayfish!" Rocky yanked Fuzz away from the hole. "The Wangflang's still there! And Hubba Blubba would nab us for sure if we went inside again."

"No one nabs the Fuzzmeister," said Fuzz, conveniently forgetting that he'd already been captured once that day.

The sirens were going berserk. The air inside the dome was thick with Gooters.

"All Oozis report to the Space Zoo!" growled Hubba Blubba through a nearby loudspeaker. "Every single one of you! The Space Penguins have escaped from the Wangflang's island and are hiding. Find them – and destroy them!"

"They think we're still inside," said Rocky.

"Bunch of idiots," said Fuzz.

"What about the Airee?" Splash insisted.

Captain Krill looked down at his slimy, dripping, green body. The others were even slimier and greener than he was.

"I have a plan," said the Captain. "We aren't four famous intergalactic heroes for nothing. Just do exactly as I tell you."

"Do you really think this is going to work, Captain?" said Splash, scooping up a flipperful of slime and smearing it across his face.

The Space Penguins had covered themselves with as much slime as they could. If you squinted, they looked like Oozis. A bit. They were roughly the same size as the green aliens at least, apart from Fuzz.

"It's all about attitude," said Fuzz. He did a little fart. "And smell."

"Got it," Rocky said, adding a smell of his own.

"We're going to slide through the main entrance," said the Captain, "pretending we're normal Oozis who've answered their chief's summons to hunt the penguins down."

"Then we're going to slide out again with the Airee and any other creatures that want to escape," checked Splash.

"You've got it," said the Captain.

"What can go wrong?" said Fuzz cheerfully.

Hundreds of Oozis were hurrying towards the main doors. The Space Penguins were swept along in a great slimy green tide, right back into the zoo again.

"You lot!" shouted an Oozi guard on a pink pathway, waving a wet green arm at the Space Penguins. "Search over there!" He pointed towards some lava pools on the opposite side of the dome. "This is no place for children," he added, looking at Fuzz.

"The Chief Oozi did say everyone," said Captain Krill, hustling Fuzz away.

"That big green bogey called me a child!" said Fuzz furiously. "I'll bake him like a clam! I'll roast him like a sea bass!"

Oozis were moving in all directions, along the winding pink paths above the islands of the Space Zoo. The Gooters' red searchlights swept over the water and the island habitats.

"The ClawBorg's still out of action," said Rocky, as they passed the great iceberg. "Look, you can see it lying at the bottom of the water."

"EEEE!"

"The Airee!" cheered Splash. "It escaped from the Wangflang's island!"

"That's because I taught it to swim,"
Fuzz boasted.

The Airee was paddling along, using its
head as a float. "EEEE!" it cried. "EEEE!"

Answering the Airee, creatures
started leaping into the water. Things
with ten legs and a hundred wings.
Beasts that looked as if they were made
out of clouds. Tiny critters with ping-
pong ball eyes and massive monsters
with no eyes at all.

The ones with wings were helping the ones without, lifting them from the water and dropping them on to the pink paths among the panicking Oozis. Creatures were running and sliding and whizzing towards the wide-open entrance doors. The chaos was perfect.

"We're over here!" shouted Splash, jumping and waving his flippers at the Airee swimming along below. "We've come to rescue you!"

FWPWPWP.

A stinky Gooter landed on the path beside the penguins.

"You!" the Oozi pilot shouted, pointing at Rocky. "Watch my Gooter. I need to refill the tank."

The pilot hurried towards a kiosk marked FILLING STATION. He picked up an empty canister marked GAS and shut the door. A horrible farty noise came out.

Captain Krill checked the fuel gauge on the Gooter. "There's still a bit of gas left. Let's fish the Airee out of the water and drop it on to a walkway. Once we do that, it should be able to reach the doors by itself."

The Gooter was easy to fly, if rather stinky. The Space Penguins squeezed together as Rocky flew the machine off the pathway and down towards the water.

"Over there!" shouted Splash.

To their horror, the Airee was almost

back at the Wangflang's island.

"After it!" said Captain Krill.

"We're seriously low on gas, Captain," Rocky warned.

"We have a mission," said the Captain. "And we're going to complete it."

Rocky roared after the Airee as it floated out of the water on to the island's rocky shore. The Airee looked up as the penguins approached.

"EEEE!" the Airee squealed, inflating its head and rising to meet them. But…

FWP… WP… P…

"Out of gas," said Rocky, as the Gooter spluttered and sank towards the Wangflang's waiting jaws. "Sorry, guys. Looks like it's barbecue time."

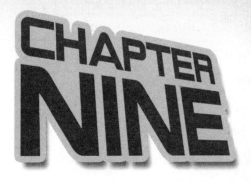

CHAPTER NINE

GLOG GOES GLUG

The Wangflang lunged with a terrible fiery roar. Flames burst across the Gooter's windscreen, and the slimy coating on the vehicle caught fire.

Two of the gas thrusters exploded, sending the Gooter shooting back up again in a mad spin.

"Everything's under control!" Rocky shouted, his feet and flippers a blur.

"WAHOOO!" cried Fuzz.

On just one spluttering thruster, Rocky

spun the flaming Gooter round in a full circle, scooped the Airee through the open cab door and steered the burning vehicle up towards the nearest walkway.

"Hold tight!" he yelled.

The Gooter bounced down on the walkway. Oozis dived out of the way into the water below as the speeding vehicle skidded and slipped along. Finally, it smashed into the filling-station kiosk beside the main doors. The Space Penguins pulled the squealing Airee on to the path and hurled themselves behind the remains of the kiosk as the Gooter exploded in a giant red gas ball.

BA-BOOOOOOM!!!

The noise and the smell were horrendous. Creatures zoomed and flapped and crawled and ran past the vehicle's burning remains. Oozi guards rushed around helplessly, trying to herd the creatures back inside the zoo and shut the doors, but they were outnumbered.

BHARGH-BRUP BHARRRGH.

The penguins saw a familiar pair of green and yellow arms raised high above the panicking crowd. The Chief Oozi was standing with Glog and his trumpeters, looking in horror at the chaos.

"My Space Zoo!" wailed Hubba Blubba. "It's ruined!"

"Time to leave," said Rocky. "Most of our slime disguise has dripped off. We're going to get spotted any minute—"

Glog pointed a green finger at the penguins. "IT'S THEM!" she gasped.

"Now?" suggested Splash.

"Just try and catch us, Glog!" Captain Krill challenged.

The alien acrobat sprang into the air, a wet blur on the pink path, and she sped towards the penguins like a bright green slime machine.

"NINJA PENGUIN!" shouted Fuzz.

He leaped into the air. His feet struck Glog's tummy.

BOING!

Fuzz landed on his bottom on the path. Glog fell off the pathway and plunged into the water below.

PLOP!

Captain Krill leaned over the side of the pathway. "Just to be clear," he told the spluttering acrobat. "I'm not fat."

"Perhaps we should rename her Glug," said Rocky.

Hubba Blubba's whole body went dark green with rage. "GET THEM!" he shouted.

The crowd parted as the guards and the trumpeters rushed towards the penguins. The Airee floated above the space mates, happily inflating and deflating its head as the penguins threw themselves on their bellies and whizzed through the doors at full speed.

The moment the penguins were outside, they heaved against the great doors until they began to close, holding back the guards on the other side.

Splash pulled a welding torch out of his toolbox to seal up the doors. Hubba Blubba's wet green and yellow mouth opened in an O of surprise.

"Enjoy your captivity, Blobberchops!" Fuzz shouted cheerily through the glass. "We did. The Wangflang's loads of fun."

As Splash welded the doors of the Space Zoo shut, the penguins were mobbed by adoring PomPoms. The other space creatures had already disappeared among the rocks and gloopy pools of Splurdj. The Airee floated gently towards the cosmic crazy-golf dome. The Space Penguins suspected that it was probably good at weightless golf.

Stroking the PomPoms, the crew of the *Tunafish* gazed through the walls of the Space Zoo and watched the captive Oozis rushing backwards and forwards. A long steel tentacle suddenly burst into view, waving around and snapping angrily.

"Those lucky Oozis," said Splash. "The ClawBorg just untangled itself."

"I hope that rude acrobat is still in the water," said Captain Krill.

"I'm dying of starvation," said Rocky. "And my eyebrows need a wash."

"Let's go back to the *Tunafish* for an ice-bath and a bite to eat," said Fuzz. "One for all…"

"And all for FISH!"

P.S.

"Nobody panic," shouted Hubba Blubba. "THIS IS ALL UNDER CONTROL."

Hundreds of Oozis ignored him and kept on panicking.

Hubba Blubba turned to Glog, who was dripping a little more than usual. "I built a way out of my own zoo, of course," he boasted. "In case something like this ever happened."

"Did you?" said Glog in relief.

Hubba Blubba pressed a button set in a panel. A ladder slid down, leading to a pretty green island directly below the walkway they were standing on.

"On that island," he said smugly, "there is a trapdoor which leads straight to Fort Gundj. Escape will be much simpler than those idiot penguins think. Follow me!"

He gripped the ladder and slid quickly to the bottom. Glog followed, together with a few guards and trumpeters.

There was a sudden scream from the Oozis still on the walkway. Hubba Blubba put his slimy hands on his hips and frowned up at them.

"What now?" he said irritably.

The Wangflang had appeared on the green island's shore, wet from a short swim across the water. It looked more furious than ever, because the ClawBorg had bitten its tail. It roared, coughing out big angry clouds of smoke. Then a bit of fire. Then a LOT of fire. It started galloping straight towards Hubba Blubba.

"OK," said the Chief Oozi, moving back towards the ladder as fast as his slimy body allowed. "EVERYONE CAN PANIC NOW."